THIS BOOK BELONGS TO

_____

_____

_____

Not Yet a Yeti

An original concept by author Lou Treleaven

© Lou Treleaven

Illustrated by Tony Neal

MAVERICK ARTS PUBLISHING LTD
Studio 3A, City Business Centre, 6 Brighton Road, Horsham,
West Sussex, RH13 5BB, +44 (0)1403 256941
© Maverick Arts Publishing Limited September 2018
Published September 2018

A CIP catalogue record for this book
is available at the British Library.

ISBN 978-1-84886-340-8

Maverick
publishing
www.maverickbooks.co.uk

George looked back inside his head.
Finally he saw it. "I want to be...

unicorn!"

Mum stopped stirring. "Are you sure?"

"Yes!" said George.
"I'm not a yeti. I'm not even
not yet a yeti. I'm a unicorn!"

As George spoke, a sparkly horn appeared on his forehead,

his arms and legs grew hooves,

and a mane and tail swooshed onto the bits
where manes and tails go.

"Derek!" Mum yelled. "You'd better come in here! George has turned into a unicorn!"

Dad let out an earth-shaking roar.

ROAR!

George took a deep breath.

"Dad? I don't want to frighten people.
I want to help them.
I'm not yet a yeti.
And I never will be."

Dad scratched his furry head. "Well," he said,
"We do love chasing hikers.

But if we keep eating them, they'll become extinct.
So, maybe WE could chase them...

...and YOU could rescue them?"

George's grandad was a yeti.

My Grandad

My Sister

His sister was a yeti.

His mum and dad were yetis.

My Mum

My Dad

All of George's family were yetis.

All of them except George.

NOT YET A YETI

WRITTEN BY LOU TRELEAVEN

ILLUSTRATED BY TONY NEAL

To you, whoever you decide to be.

George's grandad was a yeti.
His mum and dad were yetis.
His sister was a yeti.

My Grandad

My Mum and Dad

My Sister

All of George's family
were yetis.

All My Family

Me

All of them except George.

"When will I be a yeti?" George asked Grandad.

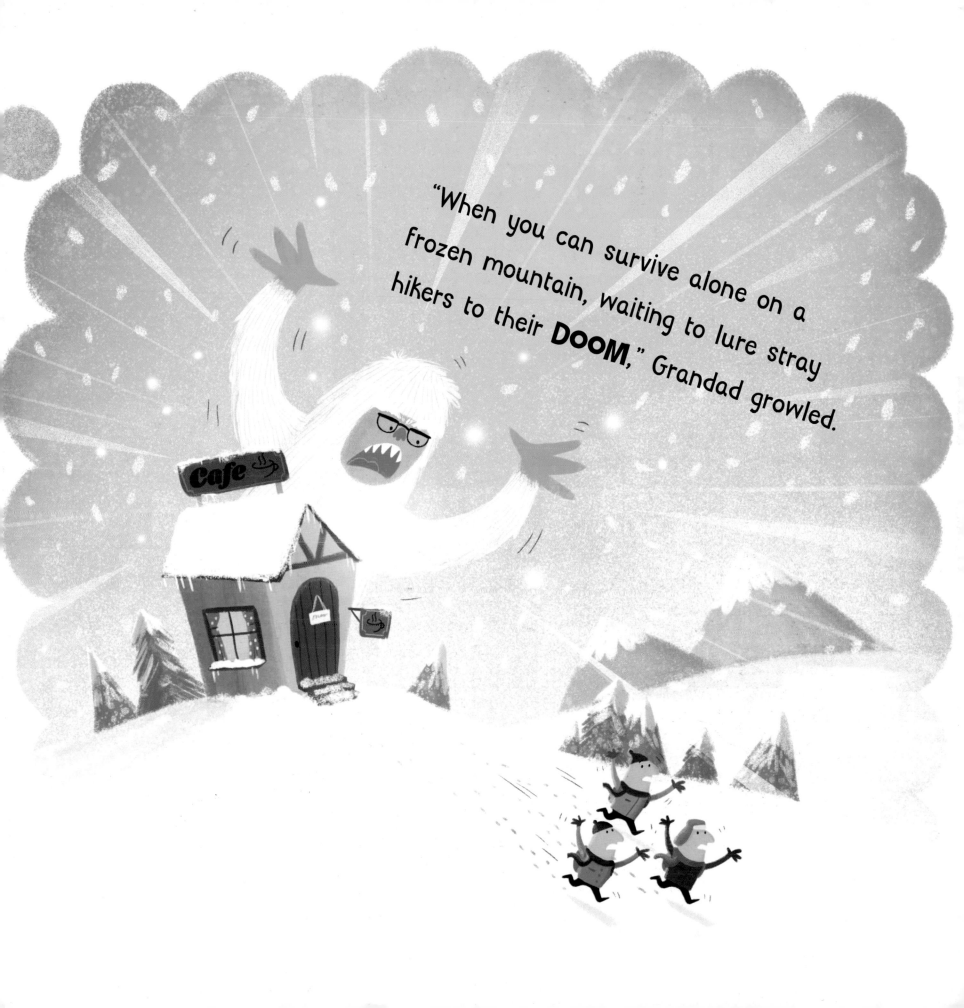

"When you can survive alone on a frozen mountain, waiting to lure stray hikers to their **DOOM**," Grandad growled.

"I don't want to lure stray hikers to their doom," said George.

Grandad put his massive paw on George's shoulder.
George nearly fell over.

"Then you are
not yet a yeti,"
Grandad said.

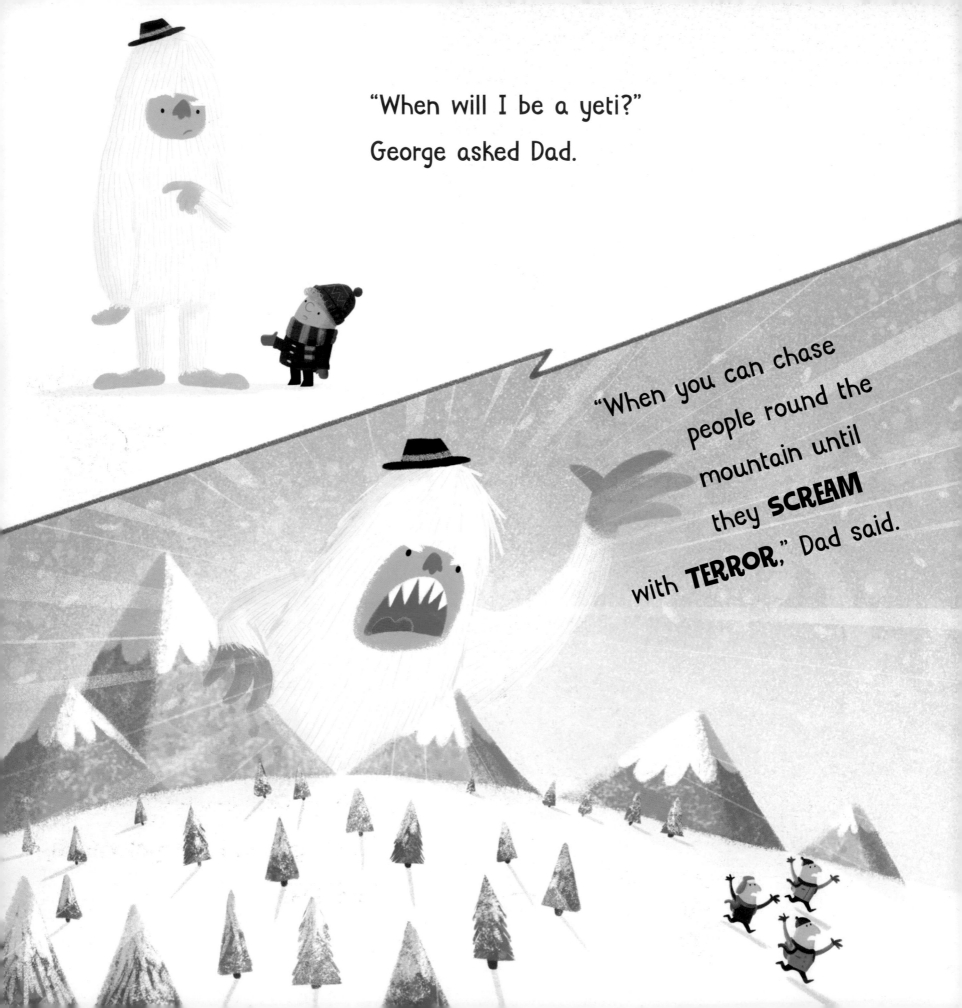

"When will I be a yeti?"
George asked Dad.

"When you can chase people round the mountain until they **SCREAM** with **TERROR**," Dad said.

"I don't want to chase people until they scream with terror," said George.

Dad hugged him.
George couldn't breathe.
"Then you are not yet a yeti," Dad said.

"When will I be a yeti? You're one already,"
George said to his big sister.

"When you can leave a footprint in the snow that makes people **GASP** with **DREAD**," Big Sister said.

"I've only got small feet," said George. "Look."

"Then you are not yet a yeti," Big Sister said,
accidentally stomping on George's toes.

"It's not fair," George said to his mum when she came back from chasing some ramblers. "I'm still not yet a yeti."

"Do you want to be a yeti?" Mum asked.

George looked inside his head for
the yeti he imagined he would be.
It wasn't there.

"No," said George.

Mum put on some soup. She hadn't caught any ramblers that day, so it was vegetable again. "Well, what do you want to be?"